A WICKED THOUGHT CROSSED HER MIND.

WHAT WOULD THEY DO, SHE WONDERED, IF SHE JUST CONTINUED? WOULD THEY KEEP WATCHING, OR WOULD THEY JOIN HER? AFTER ALL, SHE'D BEEN WISHING HER FANTASY WOULD COME TRUE, OF HAVING A VERY SEXY GUY THERE TO SATISFY HER EVERY NEED. NOW THERE WERE THREE VERY HUNKY SEXY GUYS STANDING BEFORE HER AND THEY ALL LOOKED, FROM THE BULGES IN THEIR PANTS, MORE THAN READY TO SATISFY HER.

Novels by Leigh Savage

<u>Saint Louisville Vampire Series</u>
Angel of Death
Shadows of my Past

Stand Alone Novels
Bound by Blood: Short Story Collection
Dream Dragon the Dark Side of Poetry

**Children Books written under the name
Carrie Lea Williams**

The Smile Box: A Story about Feelings
The Swan and the Rose: A Story about Inner Beauty

Thanks to all the Wicked Women and Wicked Seductions Publishing Company without them this project would never have come to be.

A Special Thanks to the lovely **Seraphina Donavan** for creating the cover art for this book.

You may find out more about Seraphina and her work here:

https://www.facebook.com/seraphina.donavan

https://www.facebook.com/pages/Seraphina-Donavan/211121168972963?fref=ts

http://www.amazon.com/Seraphina-Donavan/e/B008TCY3I6/ref=sr_tc_2_0?qid=1432400436&sr=8-2-ent

Goldi's Three Bears

By

Leigh Savage

Chapter 1

Samantha Goldi peered up at the sky. She'd been walking for hours and the sun was getting lower in the sky. It would be dark soon and she still hadn't found a clearing. With her car dead on the side of the road, her relationship in the toilet and her boyfriend in bed with a blonde, it hadn't been a good day. Now, to top everything, she wasn't sure if she was going in a straight line or just walking in circles.

Everything looked the same and she'd exhausted her phone battery without ever getting enough of a signal to make a call.

At this point even if she wanted, she couldn't find her way back to the road. She had no other choice, she thought. She would have to push on, despite being sweaty, tired and hungry. The thought of losing day light and being lost in the woods at night prompted her to hurry. As if to prove her point, she heard a distant howling. She reminded herself that there were no wolves in their area and continued onward. Of course, that didn't' stop the icy fear spiraling inside her.

Continuing along what she hoped was a path, Gold heard a rusting in the woods. Even more scared than before, she broke into a run. Jogging as fast as she could, her worthless cell phone clutched in her hand, she ran until she thought she would drop.

After what seemed forever, Goldi found a break in the trees and could finally see a clearing up ahead. To her surprise and delight, there was a cabin. No lights where on but at least, it would provide shelter.

Her panic forgotten, with one last look at her dead cell phone, she approached the cabin. The thought of shelter had given her newfound hope and energy as she made her way to the front door.

Her anxious knocking was met with silence. The need for shelter, for warmth, a place to ease her tired and aching muscles along with the hope of food, prompted her to ignore her better judgment. She tried the door and luckily, it wasn't locked.

Opening the door, she called out, "Is anyone home?" No answer came. Taking a step inside the cabin, she closed the door behind her and, after fumbling for a moment, flicked a switch, flooding the room with light. The cabin looked clean and tidy which made her hopeful that someone lived there and would return at some point. She could use the help and could only hope they would be understanding about her intrusion.

The kitchen was located just off the living room and she quickly made her way to the fridge and found some sort of sliced meat. At this point in her hunger, she didn't really care what she was eating. She took some out, tearing into it hungrily.

With her growling belly appeased, Goldi moved onto the next area of discomfort. She needed a bathroom badly. Opening the first door, she discovered a small bedroom. Closing it quickly, she moved on. It was a slightly larger bedroom. Only two doors left. Please, she thought, don't let the bathroom be outside! The next room offered a king size bed and all the furniture appeared to be hand carved. The last door provided relief. After taking care of her most pressing needs, Goldi stripped off her sweat soaked clothes and stepped into the shower. The hot water felt wonderful against her naked flesh.

After her shower, she realized two things. She hadn't looked for a towel to dry herself with and she didn't have a change of clothes. Considering the state of her clothing, there was no way she was going to put them back on without washing them first. In her brief search of the cabin, she hadn't see a washer or dryer. Standing at the bathroom sink, she washed out her clothes, after wringing them out, laid them flat to dry.

Goldi's damp skin became chilled, so she left the bathroom, still naked, in search of the large king size bed she'd seen. She told herself she would just lay down for a minute or two, just to get warm, then she would go back and check her clothes to see if they were dry. She lay down in the soft bed under the warm covers and after just a few moments, drifted off to sleep.

~~***~~

Goldi awoke, the cool air hitting her bare skin made her nipples taut. For a moment, she'd forgotten where she was. Listening carefully…all seemed quiet and she was still alone. A glance through the bedroom window showed it had grown completely dark outside. She had no idea how long she'd been asleep. Still feeling tense from the day's events, she took a deep breath and exhaled. Stretching, the covers slipped down her body exposing her naked flesh; the cool night air against her skin, creating goose bumps.

A wicked thought as to how to ease her tension crept in, but could she dare? Her hand gently traced over her nipples. Tugging on the hardened peaks, caused desire to course though her body.

Goldi felt extremely naughty lying there, touching herself in a stranger's bed. The feeling made her want to push the boundaries even more. Pushing aside the covers and any lingering doubts, she moved her hand from her nipple and began sliding down her tummy to the folds of her pussy. Wetness touched her fingertips as she dipped them inside of her pussy. Tentatively at first, but her desire quickly spread and she became more brazen.

She begun to thrust her fingers in and out of her wetness; while fondling her clit with her other hand. A soft moan escaped her lips as her fingers continued to move in and out; building in force. She closed her eyes and began to fantasize that instead of her fingers it was a sexy hunky guy — one who existed to satisfy her every desire. He would thrust his huge hard cock inside and ease the ache.

Chapter 2

Brent, Brad and Ben Bear pulled up to their cabin.

"Hey, which one of you left the light on?" Brent directed the question to his two brothers.

"Not me," Brad and Ben answered in unison.

The three of them quietly entered their home. Nothing seemed out of place until they heard soft muffled noises coming from Brent's room. Creeping toward his room, Brent opened the door silently while his brothers looked on. To their surprise, a beautiful blonde with large breasts and curves in all the right places lie naked in his bed. The sounds they'd heard hadn't been a struggle, or someone pilfering through their belongings. It'd been the sounds of pleasure as the woman on the bed brought herself to orgasm.

Brent switched on the light for a better view of the woman. Instantly, he grew hard with desire. Unable to tear his eyes away, he watched the most erotic thing he'd ever seen.

Brent saw his brother Brad reach into his pants to adjust himself, obviously as aroused by the scene as he was. A glance at Ben showed he was suffering the same discomfort. It was understandable. She was the sexiest woman he'd ever seen. The blonde froze in place. Staring back at them, she looked frightened but there seemed to be a hint of desire in her eyes.

He wanted to take a step towards the bed but was afraid he would startle her. Who she was or why she was there just didn't matter. At that moment, he simply wanted her.

Brent imagined his brothers felt the same way. It'd been far too long since any of them had a woman. Living out in the woods, they didn't often go into town and meeting women seemed to be a tricky feat. If meeting one, she usually did not want to come way out into the woods to be with them.

Brent smiled a bit, staring at her. She looked curvy all over the way he liked his women to be. Brad, was the breast man of the bunch and the perfect tits on the woman in front of them seemed to be sending him into a frenzy. As for Ben, there was nothing he loved better than going down on a woman and the lush, wet pussy on display in front of them was probably torturing him with an oral temptation.

~*~*~

When Goldi noticed the change in the lighting, her eyes had flown open in horror. Her terror now faded into a mixture of curiosity and lust as she surveyed the three incredibly hunky men standing in the doorway.

They stared at her as if she were there next meal.

With dark brown hair and dark brown eyes, they were muscular in build but each of them varied in height slightly. If they looked this sexy in their clothes, she could only imagine what it would be like to see them in the nude.

Goldi realized her hands were still touching her wet pussy. She'd stopped moving her fingers when they entered the room but never removed her fingers from inside herself. Unsure what she wanted to do, she was still burning with desire. Embarrassed at being caught pleasuring herself in their house, but at the same time, she found herself even more turned on by the way they stared at her.

Their clearly evident desire made her feel incredibly sexy. It was something she hadn't felt in such a long time. A wicked thought crossed her mind. What would they do, she wondered, if she just continued? Would they keep watching, or would they join her? After all, she'd been wishing her fantasy would come true, of having a very sexy guy there to satisfy her every need. Now there were three very hunky sexy guys standing before her and they all looked, from the bulges in their pants, more than ready to satisfy her.

It seemed to Goldi that they were at a stalemate, as no one wanted to make the first move. She raised herself up to her knees so that she was facing the doorway, giving them a full view of her naked body. Deciding to be bold and break the silence, she said, "Now that isn't fair! You guys have seen me in the nude, so it would only be fair for me to see all of you...That is, if you're up for it?"

Chapter 3

Brent, Brad and Ben all stared at one another to see if anyone objected to what she was asking. As brothers, they'd grown very good at communicating wordlessly. This wouldn't be the first time they'd shared a woman. They all nodded in silent agreement to go for it.

Brent stepped forward first. As he moved closer to the bed, he kicked off his shoes, pulled off his socks, then his T-shirt, blue jeans and finally his underwear. He stood there his cock swollen with need. He imagined her full lips moving over him and a drop of moisture beaded at the end of his dick.

Brad and Ben both came to stand beside him as they stripped. Brent watched her as her gaze roamed over them. They were all well built from the hard work it took to live mostly alone in the woods. It grew obvious from her hungry expression that she liked what she saw. He could see the dampness from her pussy glistening on her creamy thighs.

Finally she spoke, her voice husky with desire, "Are you guys going to just stand there or are you going to join me?" Brad needed no further encouragement as he moved the quickest and made his way to her side, taking her up on her tempting offer. As he knelt down beside her on the bed, taking one of her breasts in each hand, Brent looked on. He brought his lips down to one and began suckling her taut nipple while fondling the other breast.

Ben was next, moving to the bed and settling between her legs. Brent felt his cock harden further as he took in the hot scene. One of his brothers sucking at her lovely breasts while the other feasted on her sweet pussy.

Brent walked around to the other side of the bed, kneeling next to her head, his cock poised at her perfect lips. He hoped she would take his swollen erection into the warm wet folds of her mouth. He wasn't disappointed.

Closing her hand over him, she guided his cock into her mouth, her lips closing tightly over him.

He felt the vibration of her soft moan of pleasure against his swollen cock all the while her mouth continued pleasuring him.

Watching as Brad tugged her pebbled nipple between his teeth while Ben suckled at her clit, Brent savored the erotic image. It fueled his own desire as his cock slid between her full lips and her tongue swirled over the engorged head.

~*~*~

Goldi grasped his cock in her hand as she removed her mouth for a moment. She gasped in pleasure from the combination of one mouth tugging at her nipples while her clit was being sucked and licked. Feeling the fingers of the man between her thighs go deep inside of her, she moaned. It wasn't enough. She wanted more. "Ooh, more please," she moaned.

Suddenly the man who'd been feasting on her pussy rose up and grabbed her hips. Raising them slightly, he plunged his cock deep inside her. It was almost more than she could bear, feeling the warm slickness of her desire enveloping his cock as he pushed into her.

Goldi went back to sucking the big thick erection, trying to show them all the same amount of pleasure they were giving her. She felt the ache inside of her growing; igniting a hunger she never knew existed. The pleasure was making it hard for her to keep sucking on the man. She removed her mouth once more while still stroking him with her hand.

She knew the man between her thighs couldn't last much longer. His thrusts were harder, deeper and more erratic. She hovered on the edge, but still, her orgasm was just out reach when she felt the rush of spilled seed inside her.
Finished, he moved to the side.

The man who'd been exquisitely torturing her nipples took the spot between her legs. He altered the position, raising her legs, so that one lay on each of his shoulders. He entered her slowly at first.

Goldi moaned, enjoying the feel of her pussy stretching to accommodate his size. He dick seemed bigger than his the first one who plundered her, but still not as large as the cock in her mouth. He moved in and out of her faster and harder with each thrust. The man who'd been pleasuring her pussy and who'd fucked her first was now fondling her breasts, squeezing and pinching her nipples with just the right amount of force as the other one continued to fuck her.

Goldi had never done anything like this in her life, she'd never been with more than one man before, but with the intensity of this pleasure, she feared she could never go back. After this, having only one man would never be enough.

~*~*~

Brent was aching to be inside her; wanted to feel her cum on him. He wanted to make her scream in pleasure. He wasn't sure how much longer he could hold out.

Brad seemed to be in frenzy as he moved in and out of her again, and again. Watching his brother fuck her furiously, Brent pinched the base of his cock to keep from coming. It didn't take long for Brad to finish. He grunted and stilled inside her, then pulled out. He moved to the opposite side of her from where Ben sat playing with her tits.

Brent moved between her legs and used his hands to coax her to roll over onto her stomach, then he pulled her sweet, round ass into the air. With a hand on each of her hips, he gripped her tightly and pushed inside of her, stretching her even more. Even after his brothers had taken her, she felt tight around him.

Ben, who seemed to have a full raging erection once more, moved to sit in front of her. While he fucked her, Brent watched his youngest brother move in front of their lovely blonde and guide his cock into her mouth. In her current position, she could only suck the tip, but Ben compensated by stroking his hand over the shaft. She acted so eager to please and so eager to be pleased. She'd wandered into their little sanctuary and Brent wanted to keep her, he suddenly realized.

Brad still very much seemed in the game as well. He was stroking the woman's clit while Brent pounded into her. He felt her tensing around him, felt her body tightening with her release. She moved her mouth from Ben's cock, a shattered gasp escaping her lips.

Brent gritted his teeth. He felt so close to climaxing, but he wasn't going to go first. He wanted to make her come, to make her scream.

~*~*~

Goldi couldn't believe what she was feeling. Never in her life had she been so aroused. The orgasm building inside her became so intense it almost scared her. Licking and suckling on the tip of one man's dick while she watched him stroke himself and another man using his fingers to play with her clit, all the while a huge cock moved in and out of her wet pussy. It was all too much. Feeling his balls brushing against her pussy with each stroke only added to the sensation.

Abruptly, she released the cock she'd been sucking on when she felt that burning, building desire. Goldi screamed in release as she felt the third guy come inside of her. Still, he kept thrusting, his brother kept stroking her clit, playing out her orgasm until she was trembling and gasping.

The man sitting in front of her watched intently. In the next moment, she felt him go rigid at his release. Some of his cum shot out and hit her face.

The man between her legs pulled out of her, leaving her feeling empty after being filled so completely. She wiped the cum from her face as she rolled onto her back. Still breathing hard from her release, she felt stunned when the man who'd been playing with her clit straddled her. He placed his dick between her breasts, squeezing them together tightly. He began to move back and forth with his cock sliding between her tits. David, her ex, had done that once before, but she hadn't liked it then. It was different now. Seeing the intent look on his face and knowing that the other men watched, it was unbelievably erotic.

Fingers entered her pussy, still pulsing with the aftershocks of her orgasm. She couldn't even see who was touching her, she could only feel as he stroked her special spot. She arched her back and cried out in yet another release. It didn't end there. He kept hitting the spot, making her go again, and again.

Her orgasms became so intense that her eyes began to tear up from the sheer pleasure of it all. As she cried out again, the man who stroked his cock between her tits grunted, his cum shooting out, running over her throat. He then moved off her, lying down beside her. The fingers pumping into her pussy were withdrawn and she slowly came back to earth.

Goldi felt completely spent and she couldn't move even if she wanted to, nor could she think about what she'd just done. She heard the guys around her breathing heavily, as her eyes fluttered shut.

Chapter 4

Goldi awoke to find all three men sprawled out, still naked and sleeping soundly. A blush spread over her cheeks when she thought about what she did. Pushing the feeling aside, Goldi refused to feel guilty. After all, she'd never experienced pleasure like that before and she couldn't regret getting to feel that way at least once in her life. There was something powerful about having three super hunky guys all wanting her at the same time.

When she sat up, she felt sweaty and sticky. Another horrifying thought crept in. What did she look like after all this? Deciding she would quietly slip out and get in the shower to get cleaned up before any of them awakened, she moved gingerly from the bed. Her legs wobbled and she felt sore, but deliciously so.

Opening the door quietly, she slipped into the bathroom. Goldi gazed at herself in the bathroom mirror, trying to see herself the way the guys might see her. Her breasts were not perky, but large and full. David had always been eager to tell her how much she needed a boob job. She had very curvy hips and a round ass. The men who just made love to her—no, she corrected, who just fucked her—seemed to enjoy all those things David found fault with. After having three very sexy guys taking care of her every need, she felt sexy and desirable again, in spite of the constant belittlement from her ex.

Feeling better about herself, Goldi stepped into the warm shower. She wanted to look her best when those three hot, hunky men woke up.

~*~*~

Brent awoke groggy and disoriented, but it didn't take long to get his bearings. He quickly realized the gorgeous blonde was no longer in his bed. Only his brothers remained and frankly, the idea of sleeping with them without her just felt weird.

The sound of water running reassured him that she hadn't fled. Smiling, he climbed from the bed and made his way to the bathroom. He wanted to check on her, but he also wanted a little private time with her. Stepping inside, he made his way to the shower and lightly knocked on the glass door. "May I join you?" She cracked open the door, her hair wet and lying in thick ropes on her shoulders as water sluiced over her body. "Yes," she responded with a smile.

She looked nervous and uncertain as Brent stepped into the shower with her. The enclosure was small, so small that there was no way for both of them to be inside it without touching. Looking down at the beading water dripping over her luscious curves, his cock began to stir. But they needed to talk, he reminded himself. As if she'd read his mind, she began to speak, "I'm not sure what to say to you, I've never done anything like this before," her words tumbling out one after another.

The luscious beauty spoke so fast it was all he could do to keep up.

She paused a moment then added, "The short version is that my car broke down and I went into the woods to find a clearing to get a cell phone signal and then I ended up lost in the woods and it was starting to get dark when I stumbled upon your place."

Brent already suspected it was something along those lines. There really wasn't any reason for anyone to be out here otherwise. They had nothing worth stealing, but that was a choice they'd all made. A simple life seemed easier. "I'm glad you found our place and while my brothers and I have shared women before, it's never been the way it was with you." He grinned as memories of the night flickered through his mind. The erection he'd been fighting back became impossible to ignore. Between his memories and her wet and naked body in front of him, it would take a saint not to sport a hard on. "Do you know how incredible you look?"

She gazed downward, a blush staining her cheeks. Then her gaze encountered his raging erection and she looked away. "No." The admission came out a soft shy embarrassed tone, coloring her voice. "David, my ex, always made me feel like I was never good enough or pretty enough. I've never felt that beautiful and sexy until last night when I saw the look in your eyes."

It infuriated him that anyone could ever make this beautiful, sensual creature in front of him feel anything less than perfect. He stepped closer and cupped her face in his hands while looking deeply into her golden brown eyes, so she could see that he spoke the truth. "Then your ex was crazy. You are one of the most desirable women I have ever laid my eyes on," he paused a moment before adding. "What can I call you?"

"I'm Samantha Goldi, but everyone just calls me Goldi." Again, she looked away shyly.

Yes Goldilocks, he thought, it fit her well. "I'm Brent Bear, and it's been my greatest pleasure to meet you." He placed his hands on her shoulders, easing closer to her, letting her feel just how much he meant it. His cock pressed against the slick, wet skin of her belly.

~*~*~

Goldi could feel her body responding to his closeness. "And I you, Brent" She felt flushed all over; warm and achy with desire.

When Brent reached past her to grab the bar of soap his, chest brushed against her and his cock pressed against her belly. She could feel him growing even harder. He peered down into her eyes and she could see the desire in him.

It seemed to be the most natural thing in the world when his lips descended on hers. She heard the thump as the bar of soap landed on the shower floor. He tangled his fingers in her hair, tugging her head back in just the way she loved, as he deepened the kiss.

She couldn't get close enough to him. He could've been inside her and it wouldn't be close enough. Sliding her hands over his ribs, around to his back, she pressed herself tightly to him, savoring the hardness of his big body against hers.

He broke the kiss, and she whimpered in protest. The whimpering transformed into a cry of pleasure as he dipped his head to suckle her large breasts. Her sharp intake of breath as he grazed her nipple with his teeth showed him just how ready she was for him.

Brent grabbed her hips and turned her, so her back pressed against the shower wall. There was something incredibly sexy about being with someone who could manhandle her this way. Thought fled as he kissed her lips again.

Then his hands were sliding between her legs, under her bottom, lifting her until she could wrap her legs around him. She cried out as he guided his cock inside her. With one hard thrust, he was imbedded deep within her, pinning her body between the shower wall and the solid muscle of his own form.

Goldi dug her fingers into his shoulders and held onto him as she reveled in the sensation of their wet slick bodies moving against each other. The water caressed her sensitive skin adding to her pleasure as he moved in and out of her. She was going up in flames, feeling the pressure building as she came closer to her release.

~*~*~

Brent felt her body tensing against him and knew she must be close. It amazed him how quickly she got there. She was like a powder keg. He increased the speed of his thrusts until he felt her tighten around him. The soft fluttering of her sex as the muscles rippled in release nearly drove him over the edge. Then, she finally went limp in his arms.

Setting her down gently, he turned her body so that her breasts pressed against the shower wall. Bending his knees, while she rose onto her toes, he guided his cock back inside her. Entering her from behind, the tight clutch of her sex around him was a feeling he couldn't even begin to describe. Wrapping his arm around her, his hand slid between her parted thighs to tease her clit as pushed deep inside her slick folds.

Brent felt the walls of her sheath begin to contract around him again...her orgasm nearly instantaneous. He wasn't competitive with his brothers. They shared everything, but there was some small part of him that loved the fact she'd only got off on his cock.

Feeling the sharp contractions, her body milking his cock, he gave into the tension. One final thrust and he followed her over the edge.

They both stood there for a long moment breathing heavily, trying to regain their strength. He stepped back from her, so she was no longer pinned.

Goldi turned immediately to face him, looking as stunned as he felt, her legs shaking as she leaned back against the wall. Brent retrieved the soap, lathering it in his hands before rubbing it over her breasts. Her nipples were still hard little points against his palm, sensitized from their activities. Keeping his touch light and gentle, he moved his hands lower, washing between her still trembling thighs. Maybe it was ego, or maybe it was just gluttony, but he wanted her to come again.

She moaned softly as his fingers touched her sensitive flesh. It only took him moments to find that special spot. Pressing deep, curling his fingers, he stroked her there and sent her spiraling into a climax yet again.

Her hands clutched at him, her nails digging in as she spasmed against him. When her shudders stopped, her body stilled against him, her head resting against his chest.

He felt oddly protective of her, even possessive in some ways. It was crazy to feel this way when he'd only just learned her name. Looking into her honey brown eyes, he saw something there and while he couldn't put his finger on it, it made him want to get to know her, to spend time with her and most of all, he wanted to pleasure her.

In the silence, he could hear the soft grumbling of her tummy and he knew she had a hunger of a different sort. With as much as he'd like to keep her there in the shower, pressed against his body he knew she had other needs as well. "Are you ready to have some breakfast?"

"Yes." Goldi responded in a husky whisper.

It felt good, he thought, to take care of her.

Chapter 5

Goldi sat down at the table with the three brothers, whose names she'd finally learned. Brad and Ben had introduced themselves to her only a few moments after she exited the shower with Brent. She watched them working together to fix breakfast, marveling at the way they seemed to instinctively know what the other was doing.

She asked if she could help, but they insisted that she sit and relax. Using the time wisely, she tried to figure them out. Brent seemed very much a take-charge type kind of guy, whereas the other two were used to following. It made sense to her; seeing as Brent was the oldest by a few years. While Brad and Ben seemed only a couple years apart in age. Had he always been in charge of his younger brothers? Had he been able to laugh and party to have fun, or had it always been responsibility? Her thoughts were interrupted by Brad talking to her.

"Brent said that your car broke down. After we get done with breakfast, I'll take you back to your car to get your stuff and take a look at it. See if there is anything I can do."

"Oh, that would be great! I'd love to at least have a change of clothes!"

Brad flipped the pancakes, offering her a look that said he'd be more than happy to have her in no clothes at all. "If I can't do anything, we won't be able to get someone out here on the weekend. You will have to wait until Monday."

"If any of us could do anything for your car it would be Brad, he's the one who fixes things around here," Ben offered the explanation as he stirred the eggs he was cooking.

Goldi studied each of them more carefully in the light of day. They were even sexier than she originally thought last night. Brent she'd gotten to explore more closely, already. She liked what she saw and how he made her feel. They were all extremely generous lovers. Never in her life had anyone taken the time to make sure her needs were fully met. Often times with David, she'd been left still wanting.

Bringing her mind back to her original train of thought, she went back to admiring the way each of them looked wearing only their jeans. Their muscular chests rippled with each fluid movement they made. The brothers looked a bit more rugged this morning with the slight shadow of a beard covering their faces, but it seemed to only add to their masculine charm.

A random thought popped into her head and she smiled. It went well with their last name. With having a last name like Bear, it seemed natural for them to live in the woods the way they did.

Another smile gave way to a giggle. She, Goldi, had found three Bear brothers in the woods. It was so much like her favorite fairytale of Goldilocks that she couldn't stop the giggles. She hadn't tried all three beds, she thought, but she'd certainly tried all three brothers. Each one slightly different, but only one of them was a perfect fit. Brent was taller, bigger and his cock was the largest of all three of them. Brad was the medium sized brother in every way, and Ben, he was both the youngest and the smallest, but even then, his cock was still a good size, not too long, and just thick enough to feel amazing.

"What's so funny?" Brent asked the question, his eyes gleaming with amusement.

She couldn't share it yet. It just seemed too ridiculous for words. Shaking her head, she replied, "Just life. It's taken some funny twists and turns lately."

~*~*~

Brent set down coffee and juice in front of Goldi as his brother's joined them at the table as well.

Brad bringing the pancakes and Ben had the eggs for everyone.

While they were cooking, Brent set the table and set out the drinks for everyone. When they started eating, Brent took this time to find out more about Goldi. "So, tell us what brought you to our neck of the woods?" he asked with a sheepish grin on his face. Her giggles put him in a good mood. Of course, so had the mind blowing shower sex.

"Well, I guess you can say I'm trying to start over." She sighed, a small note of sadness creeping in. "I walked in on my boyfriend — now an ex boyfriend — with another woman. In the house we lived in together — right in the bed we shared." She stared down at her plate and Brent could see the doubt in her, the insecurity. She gave a little shake of her head and then met their gazes. "So, I packed some of my things and hit the road, not knowing where I was going or what I would do when I got there. I just knew I couldn't stay."

"What an ass." Brent seethes, his brothers chiming in simultaneously. He hated it when they did that.

"You deserve better than that," Brent added and his brothers nodded in agreement.

"How could a man ever do that to a woman as beautiful as you?" Brad asked.

"Well, according to him I wasn't that beautiful." Hurt flashed in her eyes. "I'm too fat, don't dress the right way, don't act the right way or speak the right way. Everything I do is just wrong, according to him!"

Brent could see she was fighting tears. The son of a bitch had hurt her, not just once, but over and over again.

Goldi continued, "I spent so much time trying to make myself into what he wanted, instead of just leaving because — because I was afraid of being on my own. I don't have any friends or family to fall back on for support. But when I saw him in that bed with another woman, something snapped inside me and I realized there were worse things than being alone. Anything had to be better than the way he was making me feel."

"There is nothing wrong with you, Goldi. You are one of the most beautiful women I have ever seen," Brad stated with sincerity.

Brent stayed quiet, because that said it all as far as he was concerned. He glanced over at Ben, who kept nodding in agreement.

Goldi shook her head and smiled at the brothers. "You guys are so sweet but I want to know about you! Why do you live all the way out here?"

"This was our hunting cabin when we were growing up. We would come out here with our parents many times to hunt and fish. We always loved spending time here," Ben explained, but then grew silent.

Brad chimed in, picking up where his brother had left off, "When our parents died in a car crash we decided to come back out to the cabin one last time before selling the place, but we all loved it so much, we just said 'to hell with it.' We sold our houses and used some of the money to update the cabin, so we could make this our full time home."

Goldi looked confused. "But what about jobs? How do you work this far away from everything?"

Brent took over then, rounding out the explanation, "We also took some of the money and invested it. It's a steady stream of income coming in from the dividends. I also build furniture out back. There's a store that sells it for me for a cut of the money and that gives us enough money to live comfortably."

"We all hunt and fish to help out and any other supplies we need, we go into town maybe twice a month to get," Ben added.

Brad finished eating and got up from table. "Let me finish getting dressed and I'll take you back to the highway to check out your car."

Chapter 6

It took no time for them to reach her car. "Shit, I must have been walking in circles yesterday!" Goldi exclaimed. "I could swear I spent hours in these woods before I found my way to your cabin.

"It's very easy to do if you don't know your way around." Brad offered, his conciliatory tone clear for her benefit. "Pop the hood."

Goldi did as he requested, sliding behind the wheel and pressing the button.

From beneath the hood, he shouted instructions, "Try to turn it on, so I can hear what it does."

Goldi turned the key but it only made a clicking noise. Brad tinkered with the motor for a few minutes and she patiently waited.

"Now try it," he called out.

Goldi turned the key again with the same result. A sinking feeling settled in her stomach.

Brad shut the hood of the car and walked toward the driver's side door.

"Is there anything you can do?" she asked.

He shook his head. "Sorry. We'll get a tow truck on Monday and have the car taken into town to be looked at. There are a couple different things it could be and any one of them will require parts and those will have to be ordered." Brad walked behind the car. "Pop the trunk and I'll grab your bags for you." Goldi did as he requested then went to the trunk as well and helped with a couple of small bags. Mentally, she was calculating the very small amount of wiggle room she had in her checkbook. Bottom line, she thought, I'm screwed, and this time…not in the good way.

~*~*~

Brad shut the trunk lid and led Goldi back through the woods. The sun was climbing higher in the sky as sweat started to drip down his forehead. He stopped for a moment to let Goldi rest. She was sweating and her damp shirt clung to her big beautiful breasts. He knew that Brent had spent some quality time with her in the shower that morning, and he'd stayed in bed like a good little brother and let him have it.

Brent worked harder than any of them and deserved a little fun. But now it was his turn. Tilting his head thoughtfully, trying to look innocent, he said, "If you like, there is a creek nearby that has a good swimming spot. We could cool off in."

Her face flushed with heat, Goldi tugged at her sweat dampened clothes as she answered, "That would be great." Leading the way, Brad shifted courses slightly, taking one of the trails that forked off the main one. He heard her gasp as they broke through the trees. It was a pretty spot, with crystal clear water that let you see right to the bottom. He laughed as she dropped her bags and began stripping immediately. He hung back, undressing more slowly, enjoying the show as parts of her jiggled and shimmied.

She dove into the water, and came back up quickly with a surprised shriek. Her breasts bobbed on top of the water, her nipples pebbled from the icy creek.

"Why didn't you tell me it was so cold?"

Brad walked to where Goldi was standing. It hadn't dawned on him that a city girl wouldn't realize how cold a mountain fed creek could be. Rubbing his hands up and down her arms to warm them, he said,. "It will take a couple of minutes to get used to it. T." She leaned into him and he felt her rock hard nipples press against his chest. Folding her into his arms, he let his body heat warm her. After a few minutes, she stopped shivering. Je looked down at her. "Better?"

"Yes, thank you." She looked up at him, their eyes locking. He could see the minute she realized exactly what was going to happen. His cock, even in the cold water, was hot and hard against her. Her pebbled nipples grew harder and he smiled. It wasn't the cold making her respond like that.

Brad laced his fingers though her hair while his other hand drifted to her round ass. He gently tugged on her hair pulling her head up so that she would expose her throat to him. His lips trailed kisses down her throat, alternately using his tongue to soothe and his teeth to gently graze her sensitive skin. Her sharp intake of breath ended on a sigh that fanned over his bare flesh. Shifting his hand from her ass, bringing it up to cup her breast, he savored the weight of it in his palm.

Unable to resist, he dipped his head down so he could suckle on her nipple. Swirling his tongue around her nipple, teasing it, he heard her moan in pleasure. Smiling, he moved to the other breast paying it the same attention.

Releasing her hair, he moved both hands to her curvy hips. Shifting them beneath her ass, he lifted her up to wrap her legs around his waist.

The tip of his cock touched the folds of her pussy. The heat of her sex on his cock while the cold water swirled around his balls was sweet torture. Slowly he lowered her, inching his cock into her. Her breasts pressed firmly against his chest as he repeated the motion. Goldi was a big girl, not too big, he thought, just right. But weightless in the water, he had free rein to fuck her however he wanted. Lifting her up until his cock was just barely inside her, he thrust deeply again, sinking into the scalding heat of her.

With Goldi's arms wrapped around his neck and her legs around his waist as he lifted her up, he could feel her pussy clenching around his cock in protest as he withdrew.

Her nails dug into his flesh and he responded by thrusting harder into her as he brought her down onto his cock. Increasing the force of each thrust, he was rewarded with her moans of pleasure. With his hands still cupping her ass, he squeezed the plump cheeks tighter, spreading them so that he could thrust deeper inside her.

She tensed against him and he knew she was close to her release. It still bothered him that he hadn't been the one to make her come. He meant to change that. Deepening his thrusts, he felt her tighten around his cock. She cried out as her pussy trembled and fluttered around his cock. It sent him over the edge with her. Holding onto shaking body for a moment, still fully inside her— Brad struggled to catch his breath. Not wanting it to be over just yet, he walked slowly to the shore, carrying her in his arms. In a soft grassy area next to the creak, he knelt down and gently laid her on her back.

Limp and sated, he finally slipped t from inside her. Looking down at her, still kneeling between her legs; she was so sexy laying there before him.

"Goldi, you're so beautiful! I have to taste you." Brad whispered the words huskily to her but didn't wait for her to respond. Lowering his face between her parted thighs, he touched his lips to her pussy. Slowly, he began to lick, suck and nibble on her tender flesh. It didn't take long for her to moan in pleasure once more as she moved her hips, pressing herself more fully against his mouth.

Goldi was shivering beneath him, gasping and crying out her pleasure as he feasted on her. Smiling against the slick folds, tasting her cream on his lips, he knew he would never get enough of her. When she slid one hand down her belly, her fingers moving over her clit, stroking herself as he thrust his tongue inside her, it was so intensely erotic. His cock sprang to life again, lengthening and thickening. He could fuck her again, he thought, as soon as she came. Then her hips were arching upward, her body tensing beneath him.

"Now, she cried out."

Quickly Brad rose up and positioned himself so he could thrust deeply into her. Her fingers still toyed with her clit, her fingertips brushing his cock as he thrust into her. It only turned him on more. He was fucking her like a horny teenager, all speed and power, racing to the finish line.

With only a few deep hard thrusts, he felt her tensing once again. Her cries were different, her body stretching taut as her hips arched up. Pressing deep, he began quick, shallow thrusts while her fingers moved furiously over her clit.

Placing a hand on her breasts, he began to tug and tease one nipple and then the other. Pinching the hardened buds between his fingers, he squeezed harder, twisting lightly. She screamed his name, her hips pumping furiously against him. Then it happened...

Her pussy clenched tight around him, then spammed sharply. A rush of clear fluid erupted from her, bathing his cock, as she cried out in release.

Brad stopped moving, stunned by what had just happened. It was the hottest thing he'd ever experienced. Goldi's hand stilled, and he could see that she was as stunned as he was. Bringing his hand down, resting it on top of hers, he used his thumb to rub the hardened nub of her clit.

"Have you never squirted before, Goldi?" he asked. His cock was hard and thick inside her, the walls of her sex still fluttering around him. He wanted to pump into her, but more than that, he wanted to see her come again.

She blushed furiously. "No," she admitted, though the word came out on a long moan.

He smiled triumphantly. "Then I was your first." With that, he could no longer hold back. Flexing his hips, he moved within her, pounding his cock into her furiously. She screamed, more of the sweet juices dripping from her flesh. Two thrusts more and he was erupting inside her, filling her with spurt after spurt of cum.

~*~*~

Goldi felt h his seed spilling deep inside her. It triggered another wave of pleasure and fresh rush of moisture as she once again cried out in release. His cock slipped from her, and even that sensation was too much, eliciting shivers and moans from her.

The feeling of emptiness it left behind surprised her, but it was only a moment. His fingers pressed into her, his thumb stroking her clit. Goldi wasn't sure she could come again, wasn't sure she could survive another orgasm. Even as she thought it, her body betrayed her. . She moved her hips meeting the movement of his fingers as they found her special spot again. The sensation was so strange, the tension coiling so deeply in her. Over and over he stroked the spot, making her cry out again and again until she thought she would die from sheer pleasure.

"Please!" She cried out weakly not sure, if she wanted him to stop or keep going.

"Once more, sweet girl. Let me see you come for me."

She had no other choice. His fingers pumped into her, his thumb circling her clit, and then she was falling. Her body shuddering as she came.

When the spasms finally halted, she met his gaze. He looked almost disappointed. "Are you upset?"

He laughed. "No. God, no. That was the hottest damn thing I've ever seen, Goldi. I'm just upset I couldn't make you squirt again."

She blushed furiously. "I've never done that before. I didn't even think it was possible."

He slipped his fingers from her, and she moaned in protest. Every part of her was so sensitive, even the slightest touch created a wealth of sensation. It was overwhelming. Goldi shivered with it, and then he was there, closing his arms around her, pressing her close to his body. His hand stroked over her back, gently, his touch soothing.

They both laid there beside each other resting and regaining their strength. It was a lazy way to spend the afternoon, but it felt heavenly.

At some point, they must have slept, because Goldi awoke disoriented. A rustling sound in the bushes, making her panic. "Brad; did you hear that?" she asked softly but there was no response. When she looked down she noticed that he was still sound asleep.

She heard the noise again this time it sounded closer. Goldi got up and grabbed her shoe. It wasn't much of a weapon, but it was all she had. Walking closer to where the noise came from, she hoped it was only a small animal she could scare away. Edging closer and closer, she screamed and fell backward when a deer jumped out from behind the bushes and went dashing through the woods.

Goldi clutched her chest, her heart racing beneath her palm, but she was relieved it was only a deer. Then another thought occurred to her. Something had scared the deer. Goldi wanted Brad. She wanted to feel safe. Whatever had scared that deer wasn't going to be scared off by her shoe.

Turning around, she jumped back when she smacked straight into a bare chest. The startled scream died away when she realized it was only Brad. "Oh, it's only you" she said on a relieved sighed..

"We better get our things and get back before it gets too late. The predators are starting to come out," he said matter of factly.

Quickly they both got dressed and grabbed the bags as he led the way back to the cabin.

Chapter 7

When Brad and Goldi approached the cabin, both Brent and Ben were waiting for them.

"Thank god you're back," Brent greeted the both of them.

"I thought I was going to have to come looking for the two of you," Ben stated.

"What's wrong?" Brad asked his brothers.

"It came back and this time, there was more than one," Brent explained. His tone disapproving.

Brad knew he was pissed, but wouldn't say anything in front of Goldi.

"I don't understand. What came back?" Goldi asked. Ben took pity at her bewildered look and explained, "There's a wolf that keeps coming round and this time, it didn't come alone, see?" He pointed to the ground where there was some paw prints.

"What are you going to do?" she asked.

Brad let Brent answer the question, it was his call after all. "We're going to find the pack and do what it takes to keep our place safe," Brent replied matter of factly.

"Someone needs to stay here with Goldi in case the wolves come back while we're out," Brad suggested.

"Ben," Brent replied. "You're a better shot, Brad. I need you with me."

Both brothers nodded in agreement.

"Alright then, Ben, please take Goldi inside. Brent and I will head on out and hopefully, be back before too long." He gave Goldi one last reassuring smile and a wink, then walked away with his brother.

~*~*~

"Come on, Goldi. Let's get you inside," Ben urged.

Goldi allowed him to lead her toward the house, but she paused at the door. "Be careful you two," she called out as she entered the cabin. She felt a shiver run down her spine as the nighttime sounds of the woods filtered in.

Ben must have felt her shiver as well because he walked over to the fireplace and stoked the banked blaze before adding more wood.

She sat on the sofa watching his movements intently, admiring the way his muscles looked as he moved. The light of the fire seemed to define his muscles even more with each movement. When he walked towards her, she found herself following the trail of his chest hair to the point where it disappeared into his jeans. He stopped in front of her, just within reach. She couldn't help herself. Goldi reached up to undo his jeans, wanting to see all of him. She didn't want to think about how scary the woods could be. She only wanted to feel safe in his arms.

With his jeans gone and his cock hard in front of her, Goldi took him in hand. She smiled at his sharp intake of breath. His heavy breathing turned into a harsh groan as she closed her mouth over the head of his cock, sucking him deeply. She'd gone down on him the night before, but she'd been distracted by all the wonderful things they'd been doing to her. Getting to be with each of them individually, in addition to their little group encounter, felt incredible.

Swirling her tongue around the head of his cock, she felt his fingers tangle in her still damp hair, holding her head in place. She had no intention of going anywhere. Bobbing her head up and down, she took him even deeper, loving the sensation of his cock sliding over her tongue. He tasted like heaven to her.

Goldi moaned in protest as Ben stepped back, pulling his cock from her mouth. But then he was kneeling on the floor in front of her, pulling her legs over his shoulders. With his face buried between her thighs and his tongue lapping at her wet pussy, she could hardly complain. He licked, sucked and nibbled her clit with a heady mix of enthusiasm and skill. She couldn't hold back her helpless moans of pleasure.

He pressed his tongue firmly against her clit, curling around it.

"More," Goldi moaned as she arched her back, pressing herself more firmly against his mouth.

Ben lay back on the floor, pulling her down on top of him.

Goldi followed eagerly and immediately guided his cock into her wet, waiting pussy. She moved slowly at first, enjoying the sensation of being the one in control. Watching his changing expression as she moved up, then down slowly over his cock as it stroked her burning need.

With his hands on her breasts, his fingers tugging expertly and her taut nipples, she felt her control starting to waiver. Her movements became faster, jerkier. Then one of his hands slid between them, his fingertips rubbing against her clit as she rode him.

Goldi felt her pussy tightening, quivering and then once again, she was crying out in release. She was still spasming around his cock when Ben rolled her onto her back and thrust so hard and deep inside her, she actually saw stars.

~*~*~

Ben loved the way her lush body felt under the weight of his own. He loved how he felt inside of her and he loved the way she responded to his every touch, kiss and thrust. Half-afraid about how maybe, he just loved her, he drove into her again as he buried his face between her large breasts.

He didn't want to come immediately. Needing to hold back, to give her another release, he forced himself to slow down. He stilled inside her, once again bringing his hand between their bodies to strum her soft, little clit. But his Goldi seemed primed and ready. Tapping his finger on that little bud just a few times, she was coming again, her sheath closing around his cock tighter than a fist.

Ben thrust into her again, spearing through the clenched muscles of her sex until he was seated deep inside her. Then, he let go. His balls drew up, taut and aching. Gazing down at her, flushed from sex, her lips parted on a soft cry and her nipples hardened from her own pleasure, it pushed him over edge.
He came in thick spurts, his cock trembling inside her with each rush of fluid. Her hands trailed over his back, then up, running through his hair as he collapsed on top of her. With his head pillowed on her perfect breasts and his cock still deep in her sweet pussy, it was perfection.

After a few minutes, Ben lifted his head and rolled off Goldi, bringing her with him, so she lay beside him. He tilted her face so he could kiss her sweet lips, her body pressing against his as he deepened the kiss. He brought his hands around her body and grabbed her thick luscious ass.

She moaned softly into his mouth.

Enjoying her response, Ben released the kiss and moved her rolling her onto her stomach, giving him full range as he positioned himself between her legs. He took an ass cheek in each hand and brought his face down so that he could nibble on her ass cheek. She moaned loudly with pleasure while moving against his lips. Hearing her moans, he took his fingers and dipped them into her wetness. He enjoyed the feel of her slickness on his fingertips. It shouldn't have been possible, but he felt himself growing hard as she moved against his fingers. Removing his fingers, he lifted her up slightly, so she was on her knees. Then, with a hand on each hip, he entered her hard and quick. His balls slapped against her pussy and his fingers dug deeply into her hips as he fucked her from behind.

Ben pounded into her harder and faster until he heard her cry out in release, yet again. A warm spurt from her quivering pussy covered his cock. Looking down at her beautiful ass, he wanted to see his cum on her skin. Pulling out, he grasped his cock, jerked once on it and then gave a harsh growl as the pearly fluid shot out onto her white skin. Unbelievably, he was still hard. Goldi collapsed back onto the floor, her body trembling.

Ben laid down, half on top of her, his still hard cock pressed against her hip.

Her eyes widened. "Again?" she asked breathlessly. He chuckled. "There are some benefits to being the youngest...I can go all night."

She shivered against him. "One of the benefits of being a woman is that I can too."

Ben gently glided his hands down her side, tracing the curve of her hips, then over the roundness of her ass…dipping down, so he could touch her wetness. Sliding his fingers deep inside her, he stroked her until she writhed against him in heated desire.

He might be the youngest and going all night wasn't a problem, but the damn carpet was. It was playing hell on Goldi's soft skin. Seeing the marks on her lovely white skin, he tugged her up with him and onto the couch. He sat first, then tugged her down to straddle him, facing him. While his cock glided into her dripping pussy, her lush breasts bounced in front of his face. Clasping his hand over one breast, he urged her forward until he could take the taut bud of her nipple into his mouth.

She didn't thrust up and down on him, but rocked gently. Flexing her hips, her ass moving against his thighs as she rode him. Her breasts seemed so sensitive that the slightest touch made her whimper. With one hand squeezing a abundant breast, the other hand cupping one delicious ass cheek, Ben indulged his own urges. Lifting his hand from her ass, he brought it back down quickly, the sound of the smack resonating through the cabin. Goldi jerked, then moaned. "Again," she urged.

He complied, spanking her hard and fast while she rode his cock. Three sharp slaps and she was coming, her body quivering against him, her arms wrapped tightly around his neck. He followed her climax, spilling inside her, his cum shooting into her pussy.

Goldi went limp against him and Ben could tell from her even breathing she'd fallen asleep. Carefully, he maneuvered himself, so he could carry her to his room and gently laid her down on his bed. Crawling in next to her, he snuggled up against her and soon fell asleep, cradling her in his arms.

Chapter 8

Goldi wasn't sure what exactly woke her up at first, as she looked around; she was no longer in the living room but had been carefully tucked into bed next to Ben. Getting up, she walked into the living room and noticed how the fire had almost burned out and a chill seemed to be settling in.

Then, it became all too clear what awakened her. She could hear the howling of the wolves. A quick glance into the other bedrooms showed her that neither Brent nor Brad were at home. Worried that something was wrong, she walked back into the bedroom and touched Ben lightly. Bending down close to his face, she said softly, "Ben, wake up; your bothers haven't returned yet; I think something might be wrong."

Ben awoke quickly, sitting up in bed. "What is it?" he asked still looking drowsy.

"It's really late and your brothers still haven't returned," Goldi spoke in a rush, her fear making the words tumble out, "And, I can hear the wolves—something isn't right."

Ben glanced toward the window at the darkness outside. Goldi could clearly see his concern was as great as hers.

Immediately, he rose from the bed and dressed swiftly. "What are you going to do?" Goldi asked.

"I'm going to go look for my brothers. It's too late for them to still be out. They'd be back by now if something wasn't wrong."

Goldi got up and walked over to one of her suitcases. Pulling out some clothes, she dressed hurriedly as well.

"What are you doing?" Ben demanded.

"I'm not staying here by myself while you go out into the woods looking for your bothers! I'm coming with you."

"It's not safe for you."

They'd done so much for her, she wasn't going to sit back and do nothing when they might be hurt, or worse. "I'm going and that's that," Goldi put on her shoes.

As if realizing it was pointless to argue, Ben shrugged. "Make sure you stay next to me the whole time."

Goldi nodded in agreement. The last thing she wanted was to be alone in the woods again. She watched Ben grab a backpack full of stuff from his closet along with a couple of flashlights and a gun. The gun gave her pause, but it was necessary, she knew. If it wasn't dangerous out there, Brad and Brent would have already been home. Steeling herself and ignoring her fear, Goldi followed him outside into the dark woods.

~*~*~

Brent knelt down next to Brad, checking his leg to see if the bleeding had finally stopped. He breathed a sigh of relief to see the blood had congealed. They were too far from the cabin for him to carry his brother all the way home. Brad sure as hell wasn't able to walk on that leg. It would only cause it to start bleeding again, and he couldn't risk it. He'd already lost too much blood.

Brent sighed. He couldn't leave Brad out here in the dark to fend for himself, injured and weak. They would simply have to wait until morning, he decided. Then he could go back and get Ben to help him. For the night, he would keep watch while Brad slipped in and out of consciousness. Between the pain and the blood loss, he seemed groggy and disoriented even when he was awake.

The howling of wolves in the distance had him reaching for his gun, checking it again, to make sure it was loaded and ready. Turning back to the fire, Brent threw some more sticks onto the blaze, hoping the flames would detour any predators from coming closer.

~*~*~

Goldi followed closely behind Ben as they made their way through the woods.

Every now and then, Ben would stop and examine the ground or bushes, then they would continue on.

She had no idea what he might be looking for, but she followed just the same.

At last, through the trees, they could see a dim glow. It had to be a fire burning in the distance.

Ben picked up his pace, all but running toward the light. She followed behind him, realizing in that moment just how afraid he'd been for his brothers.

Brent must have heard their approach. By the time they cleared the trees, he stood in front of his injured brother, using his own body as a shield.

It hit Goldi then. There'd never been anybody in her life who would have done that for her.

When he recognized them, Goldi saw the relief passing over his handsome face, but she also saw the fear. Whatever happened to Brad, it must be bad.

"Damn I'm glad to see you two!" Brent exclaimed.

"What happened?" Ben asked, moving closer to his brothers, kneeling beside Brad's prone form. .

"Brad's leg got caught in a hunters trap." Brent turned to Goldi, offering her an explanation, "We're the only ones who hunt out here and we never use traps. It never occurred to us to look for something like that. Whoever's been out here hunting on our grounds have laid down all kinds of traps."

"That has to be what's upsetting the wolves," Ben suggested.

While Goldi listened to the brothers talking, she became aware of a rustling sound behind her. She turned and walked a little closer to the bushes expecting to see a small animal scurry out. Instead, she saw the eerie glow from the eyes of a much larger animal. They stared back at her intelligently and she simply couldn't move.

Goldi stood frozen to the spot, her eyes locked with whatever creature who stayed hidden behind the bush. She thought about calling for help, but was so mesmerized by the glowing eyes, she couldn't do anything.

The animal slowly emerged from the bushes, moving closer to her. The solid white wolf looked magnificent, and large enough to be intimidating.

Goldi knew she should be scared, but instead she felt calm as the wolf approached.

Some instinct compelled her to kneel, to extend her hand toward the majestic animal. The wolf sniffed her outstretched hand, going so far as to lick one of her fingers.

Goldi heard footsteps behind her, too heavy to be Ben's, which only left Brent. A glance behind her confirmed it. Without saying anything, she turned back to the wolf, but it must have retreated into bushes. With its head tilted, it stared at her as if waiting for her to follow. Following her instincts, Goldi took a step towards the wolf.

"Goldi, don't!" Brent whispered forcefully.

Goldi glanced at him, "Don't worry," she said as she turned and took off into the woods.

"Damn!"

She could hear Brent's curse, and the sound of him following behind her.

~*~*~

Goldi followed the wolf to a cave. The animal paused at the entrance, looking back at her expectantly. Inside, the cave seemed damp and dark while she noted her flashlight wasn't nearly as bright as she wished it to be. The chilled air raised goose bumps on her flesh. Walking deeper into the cave, she could hear a whimpering sound a short distance ahead.

The white wolf stopped. On the ground beside him was a black wolf, soft whimpers escaping the obviously injured animal. Realizing it was hurt, Goldi knelt down and using her flashlight, examined the wolf. She stopped when she noticed a mangled front leg.

"Goldi are you in there?" Brent cried out.

"Yes!" Goldi called out, trying to get a better view of the wolf's injury. She'd have to get him out of the cave, but figuring out the means would be no picnic. Still struggling with that, she heard Brent enter the cave. Without looking at him, Goldi explained what she'd seen, "The wolf's leg is all bloody, probably from the same kind of trap that got Brad. It's hard to tell how deep the cuts go. I really need to get it cleaned up, so I can see it better."

Brent took her arm, speaking slowly and calmly, but urging her toward the exit. "Goldi, that wolf could hurt you. You have to be more careful."

Goldi peered up at Brent and spoke with a certainty she didn't understand herself, "They won't hurt us. They need our help, Brent. Don't ask me how I know, because I can't answer that. It's just something I feel when I look at the wolves. I just know that they don't mean us any harm!"

He stared at her as if she were crazy, before shrugging and muttering, "What the hell." Stooping down beside the injured animal, one eye on the white wolf standing guard, he surveyed the injury as Goldi looked on.

She heard his indrawn breath when he saw the wound. "This is bad. We need to get the wolf back to the camp. There, I have supplies in the backpacks we can use to clean this up."
"It's going to be all right! We're going to take you some place where we can help you," Goldi implored in her most soothing voice as she gently picked the black wolf up into her arms.
The injured wolf didn't growl or protest, it simply whimpered as it lay in her arms.

"Follow us," Goldi urged the white wolf. With protective as the wolf behaved of its injured companion, she didn't think it would be an issue.

~*~*~

While they walked, Brent couldn't help but admire the bravery Goldi had shown. Most women would never have gone out to the woods at night to look for him and his brother. Even now, watching the way she acted with the wolf, carrying it gently and talking to the animals as if they were human, she amazed him. .Even more amazing, the wolves responded to her as if indeed, they understood her.

Could he dare to think for a moment that he'd finally found a woman who would be at home in the wilderness? Someone caring and passionate who would stay with them?. He couldn't help but smile at the thought of it. Reminding himself not to let his dreams make him forget the other possibility—the one where she walked out of their lives forever.

Was he being selfish wanting her to stay? Could she truly be happy living with them? She deserved more, in terms of physical comforts, but no one would ever treasure her the way he and his brothers would.

Determined to enjoy the time he would have with her, he pushed those thoughts aside. Once her car was repaired, the choice would be hers. Still—a spark of hope remained, burning deep down inside of him.

~*~*~

Goldi sighed with relief when they finally made it back to the campsite.

Ben was pacing nervously while Brad still lay unconscious. "Were did you two run off too; you had me worried…" he trailed off, stunned at the sight of the wolves. "It's hurt," Goldi said, gently laying the wolf down next to the fire. Brent went straight to the backpack, digging through it for supplies. When he found what he needed, he moved closer to Goldi and knelt beside her, handing her a bottle of water. Without instruction, Goldi uncapped the bottle and poured the water over the injury, washing the wolf's leg. Taking the rag Brent handed her, she gently dabbed the wounds to see the injury better. Working together, they doctored the wounds.

It felt so right, taking care of the animals with Brent by her side. Everything felt better with him beside her. It frightened her just how much. "We need to get these wounds bandaged and then get Brad home," she suggested.

Brent nodded. "Between Ben and I, we can carry him back to the house."

Chapter 9

3 weeks later

Goldi spent the time while her car was being repaired by helping Brad to be able heal and get him moving again. During that time, Brent and Ben combed the woods searching for any remaining traps and disarming them.

Her time seemed to be running out and she knew it. Wishing things could stay this way forever wasn't helping her come to terms with the idea of saying good bye.

Brent, Brad and Ben were kind, gentle, caring, loving and most of all, they were everything she ever wanted in a guy. A sad smile crossed her face as she heard them moving around in the other room. Her three Bears were heading into town for the afternoon. She'd told them she wanted to stay behind since she wasn't feeling good. Her stomach was in knots and had been for days.

Nerves, she told herself, since they might come back with her car. Secretly, she hoped it wouldn't be ready. After all, her broken down car was her excuse to stay.

Goldi told herself it was crazy to feel the way she did about them. She needed a distraction, something to take her mind off her inevitable departure. She knew the brothers would take awhile as they were loading their truck with the handmade furniture today.

Forcing herself out of bed, she made her way into the kitchen to fix breakfast. Opening the door to the fridge, the smell from last night's leftovers became over powering. Slamming the fridge closed, she ran to the bathroom.

After tossing her proverbial cookies, Goldi splashed water on her face. A glance in the mirror showed her how she still looked like hell. Walking into the bedroom, she rifled through her bag looking for any stray medication that might settle her stomach. All she found was a stockpile of feminine hygiene products. Goldi felt a cold sweat break out on her skin, one that had nothing to do with being sick and everything to do with the quantum equations of reproductive math that had just gone through her head. Hurriedly, she ran outside to find the brothers to let them know she'd changed her mind. She was going into town with them after all.

~*~*~

Brent parked the truck at Matt's Auto Repair which shared space with the convenience store. Everyone piled out of the truck, but when they went inside, no one stood at the counter for the repair shop.

"I'm going to go look at the store for some flu medicine," Goldi called out, crossing the parking lot..

"That's fine; I'll wait here for the repair man," Brent responded.

Goldi entered the store, the little bell tinkling overhead making her self-conscious. A glance back outside showed that none of the guys were paying any attention to her. She turned down the medicine aisle with its small supply of feminine hygiene products. Thanking the lord for trusting souls who didn't keep pregnancy tests behind the counter and force panicky women to ask for them, she grabbed a box and took it straight to the cashier. Paying in cash, she asked, "Where's the restroom?"

The cashier pointed to the back corner of the store, a smug smile on his face.

Ignoring him, Goldi tucked the item under her arm and headed straight there. Once inside, she locked the door and opened the box with trembling hands.

Skimming the instructions, more for peace of mind than because she didn't know how to pee on a stick, she did the deed and waited. Sitting there staring at the test, her heart pounded nervously as she watched two lines slowly appear, forming a giant plus sign in the tiny little window.

In shock, Goldi began cataloguing what she needed to do. Her car might be ready today, which meant running was an option. Immediately, she scratched that. They had a right to know, she felt, but she couldn't just drop the news and then take off.

She needed time to figure out how to tell them — one of them was going to be a dad. But which one, and how weird was that going to make it for everybody? Sitting on the toilet in the tiny store, Goldi dropped her head in her hands and tried to make sense of the myriad emotions swirling through her.

She'd already tried to come to terms about leaving. It wasn't fair to them to have to share her and it would be better to get out now had one of her many arguments. But it wasn't only about protecting them. She also wanted out before she fell too hard and got her heart broken when they decided they could no longer be involved with the same woman. Tears came to her eyes; she covered her face with her hands. Goldi simply sat there and cried until she heard a knock at the door.

"Goldi are you ok?" Ben asked. "The cashier told me you came in here."

Wiping away the tears, she lied, "Yes, I'm fine." Splashing water over her face, she exited the bathroom.

If Ben noted her red and puffy eyes or suspected she'd been crying, he kept his mouth shut about it. But he did hug her, enfolding her in his arms.

For a split second, his consoling her, led Goldi to feel that everything would be okay.

She stopped at the counter next to Brent who'd already been talking to the repair man. "So, what's the status?" Goldi asked, hoping her voice wasn't too shaky.

"I'm sorry, ma'am. But one of the parts was on back order, so I'm waiting for it to come in. I'm going to need a couple more days," he informed her.

She sighed, half in relief and half in frustration, as she turned to the brothers, "Alright then, let's go."

Heading back out to the truck, Brad noticed that Goldi hadn't picked up anything for the flu "Goldi, weren't you going to get medicine?"

"I'm feeling much better now; I think it might have been something I ate," Goldi offered, hating herself for lying to any of them.

While they walked to the truck, Goldi tried to look on the bright side. At least she'd be able to take her time and figure out the best way to drop this bomb on them. She had no idea how they would take the news but she couldn't take off and never tell them about the baby. It just wouldn't be right. She needed to at least, give them the information and whatever they decided would be up to them.

Goldi wasn't going to hold any of them responsible. The last thing she wanted was to force a child on a man who wasn't ready for one. They didn't deserve that and the baby didn't deserve it either. Whatever they decided, she would respect their decision.

Distracted by heavy thoughts, Goldi stayed silent on the long ride back to the cabin.

Chapter 10

Goldi had gone to lie down after returning to the cabin. The brothers sat down together, gathering at the table. They all knew something was terribly wrong, but Brent was the first one to address it. Glancing at the closed door to the bedroom where Goldi rested, he blurted it out, "I don't want her to leave."

"I feel the same way," Brad responded.

"Me too," Ben seconded.

"We came close today to losing her. If her car had been ready, she might have walked out forever," Brent stated.

"I can't believe we almost lost her and we never took the time to sit down and talk about how we feel about her," Ben added.

"I guess it took us taking her to the repair shop to make it seem real. After all, it's been like a dream since she came into our lives. And to be honest, we've been so damn busy with the wolves and the traps, we haven't really took the time to even think about her leaving us," Brad noted.

"I think I'm falling in love with her, that's crazy isn't it?" Brent asked his brothers as he ran his fingers through his hair. He continued on before they could even respond, "It's way too soon to feel this strongly for her."

"If it is, then I'm crazy too," Brad piped in.

"Me three," Ben added.

Brent stared at them, his expression serious. "If she stayed, could we really do this? Could the three of us share her forever?"

"Yes," Ben replied without hesitating. "We share everything. We always have. This thing with Goldi...What's important is making her happy, and the three of us together do that. We probably could individually, too, but why should we? We each give her something different...something that she needs. And by herself, she's everything that we need."

"Then it's settled, over the next couple of days, let's find a way to ask her to stay," Brent announced with determination.

"Agreed!" Brad and Ben answered at the same time.

~*~*~

Goldi was the last one to come to the table for supper. Her Bears had let her sleep until everything was ready. She'd laid there most of the time thinking about how she could tell the brothers the news. Should she tell them at dinner or after dinner? What should she say?

Everything she worked out in her mind evaded her now, when she actually sat there in front of them. Her stomach was in knots and her hands were trembling slightly as she reached out to grab her drink.

"Goldi, are you feeling alright?" Brad asked.

"You've barely said a word." Ben's voice seemed laced with concern. "You haven't touched your food."

Goldi had been so deep in thought she hadn't realized she'd been staring at her plate.

The guys had already almost finished their dinner.

"Goldi you look pale; maybe we should take you to the doctor," Brent suggested.

"No! That's not necessary really," Goldi answered.

"Something isn't right, Goldi. You haven't felt good the last couple of days and you don't seem to be getting any better," Brad stated with concern marring his features.

"Please let us help you? We care for you a great deal and want you to be well." Ben squeezed her hand gently.

"At least let us take you to the doctor, so he can let us know what's wrong," Brad implored in a pleading voice.

Goldi decided that now would be as good of time as any to tell them the truth. "I already know what's wrong. I was planning on telling all of you later tonight but I just don't—know how to break the news gently." Goldi gazed at each of them, terrified of what she was about to say and of how they would respond. Saying it made it real. "I'm just going to come out and say it—I'm—pregnant. And it's going to be a baby Bear."

"Are you saying that one of us is the dad?" Brad asked.

"Yes, that's what I'm saying." Goldi took a deep breath before continuing, "Now, I want you all to know up front, I'm not expecting anything from you. I thought it was only right that I tell you."

"Stop right there," Brent interjected. He didn't sound angry, but he did sound very firm. "The baby is one of ours. As far as I'm concerned, it's all of ours and I personally can't wait to be a dad."

"I agree," Brad and Ben sated at the same time.

"Are you sure?" Goldi asked.

"I'm sure," Brent said firmly.

"We're sure," Brad corrected. "We're all in this together."

"Me too, for what it's worth? I've been sure since the first day we laid eyes on you," Ben finished off.

Relief overwhelmed her. Fighting back tears, Goldi tried to stay focused on the plans that needed to be made. "Alright. This week I will start looking for a job and a place to live in town."

"Nonsense! You're going to live here with us and let us take care of you and the baby," Brent offered.

"Yes, that way we can be a family," Brad added.

"I couldn't! It's too soon for me to move in with you guys—you don't really know me," Goldi responded.

They all laughed at that. "Goldi, we know every inch of you. But beyond the physical, we know how you make us feel...Taking care of you won't be a burden. It'll be a reward." Ben nodded his head.

"Really?" Goldi asked with tears streaming down her face.

"Really! Even before we knew about the baby, we didn't want you to leave us. Earlier today, when we thought you might be leaving us for good...we realized none of us wanted that," Brent explained.

"We were so relieved when your car wasn't ready because that gave us time to try and convince you to stay with us," Brad added.

"And to tell you we are falling in love with you," Ben finished.

Could it really be that they felt the same way about her as she'd been feeling about them? "I think I'm falling in love with all of you too. I just didn't think it was fair to each of you; for me to love all of you! I thought you each deserved a woman who would love each of you individually, so you wouldn't have to share her."

"And we were worried that you would never want to live out in the wilderness with us and that you would never be happy being with all of us," Brad replied.

"We've never met a woman before who fit so well with our way of life and wouldn't try to pull us apart," Ben added.

"What we're trying to say, Goldi…is that you're perfect for us and we think we're perfect for you. We want to make you a Bear…" Brent proclaimed, kneeling down in front of her. "I know you can't marry all of us, but take our name and stay with us. Let us love you and the baby for the rest of our days."

By the time Bren finished his unconventional but wonderful proposal, Brad and Ben were there beside him, kneeling in front of her while offering her more than she'd ever dreamed of.

Goldi felt so happy. Who would have ever guessed that breaking down in the middle of nowhere, deep in the wilderness, she would end up finding love? "Yes!" Goldi answered excitedly.

Brent stood up in front of her and pulled her up from her seat. When he took her into his arms so he could carry her into his bedroom, his two brothers followed behind him. Goldi knew she was the luckiest woman in the world to have three magnificent men who would treasure her.

Chapter 11

Gently, Brent laid her down on the bed and kissed her deeply. His fingers undid the buttons on her blouse, pushing the fabric to the side. He reached into her bra and pulled her breasts free from their restraints. He fondled one of her breasts as his kiss deepened.

Brad knelt down on the opposite side of her and took her other breast into his mouth bring her nipple to a tight taut peak. Ben undid her pants and tugged until he pulled them and her panties from her body at the same time. He knelt between her legs, burying his face into her pussy, licking and sucking on her clit while he slid his fingers deep inside her.

Goldi moaned in pleasure but the sound seemed to be muffled by Brent's eager lips. She tried to reach up and pull at Brent's jeans, but he grabbed her hands and placed them over her head. With only one of his large hands holding both hers in place, Goldi felt small and delicate. Each of her Bears was strong and powerful, and all of them wanted to please her. The very thought sent a rush of heat pooling to her pussy, her juices coating Ben's fingers as he pumped them inside her.

Goldi moved her hips, pushing her pussy more firmly against Ben's mouth. When he pulled back, Ben's lips and fingers leaving her, she felt empty inside. Her cry of disappointment altered abruptly, turning into a cry of pleasure as Ben pushed his cock deep inside of her, filling her completely.

He moved slowly at first, but Goldi urged him to quicken his pace with the movement of her hips. With Ben fucking her, Brent and Brad both stepped away from the bed, undressing as she watched them and the sight of their well-built bodies and hard erections nearly made her come right then. When they returned to the bed, one of them kneeling on either side of her, Goldi grabbed a rock hard cock in each of her hands.

Gliding her fingers up and down their hard shafts, she enjoyed the way each of their cocks responded to her movements. Ben pulled out of her, urging her to roll over to her stomach. When she did, Brent and Brad moved, so they sat at the head of the bed and both of their rock hard cocks were right there in her face. Ben pushed deep inside of her once more. Goldi moaned at the feeling of his cock spearing into her wetness. He grabbed her hips in his hands, thrusting harder and deeper. Eager to please her other lovers while Ben pleased her, Goldi t moved her mouth over Brent's cock, sucking lightly before moving to Brad's. Back and forth between their two hard cocks, sucking and nibbling at each one in turn while her hands slid with a brisk motion on each alternating cock, until the pleasure from Ben became too much. The pressure built inside her. Goldi threw back her head and cried out in release, just as she felt Ben come inside of her. The hot spurts of his seed caused her to have yet another release. Breathing heavily for a moment, she lay there on her stomach.

Brad moved between her legs, his hands trailing over the plump curves of her ass. Any other time, she would have been embarrassed, but she was too satisfied to care. Then, his palm came down hard, smacking one ass cheek. The burn on her skin was instantaneous and it ignited another burn altogether. Her pussy clenched and a fresh rush of moisture greeted each sharp slap from his hands.

Goldi couldn't hold back her moans of pleasure as he spanked her bottom. Then, he was thrusting his cock into her, filling her up with it while he continued to spank her. She came instantly, her pussy clasping tightly around his hard cock, milking him with each shuddering spasm.

Then Brent kept thrusting his big cock into her mouth, forcing it deeper while Brad fucked her from behind. Ben was beside her, his hands surprisingly gentle as he toyed with her breasts and then fondled her clit. The difference between them, Ben so gentle with her, while Brad was rougher, and Brent was just dominant, seemed to be more than she could take.

The familiar tightness settled in her belly, drawing deep. Brad thrust deeper, his cock hitting that one special spot which always sent her over the edge. A rush of fluid escaped her, drenching his cock, running over her thighs as she shuddered beneath him. Brent's cock slipped from her mouth as she screamed in release.

Brad surged into her once more and then she felt the hot rush as he came deep inside her. Hot, sticky, messy and Goldi loved every second of it.

~*~*~

Brent pulled Goldi up so ended up sitting on his lap. Her thighs were wet against his, her pussy juices coating her skin. It turned him on even more. With his hand, he guided himself inside of her as she straddled him. She lowered herself onto him slowly, taking his cock deep. She didn't stop until he completely filled her, his balls resting against her sweet ass.

Taking one of her breasts into his mouth to suckle it, he slid his down to her ass, gripping each cheek firmly, spreading them apart. His cock nudged just a bit deeper inside her then. Flexing his hands on her plump cheeks altered the pressure of her tight pussy on his cock. She cried out, arching against him. He smiled against her breast, taking it deeper, sucking her nipple harder while she clutched at his shoulders.

Brent then lifted her slightly, raising her up, only to lower her again, sliding his cock in and out of her pussy with slow, deliberate strokes. It didn't take long for his Goldi to come, yet again. She was always ready for them, eager. She shuddered and gasped against his neck while her pussy fluttered deliciously around his cock.

He needed more, he thought. More control. Rolling her onto her back, coming down on top of her, he plunged fully inside her. Pulling out, he drove into her again. Over and over, he filled her, hard and deep. She kept screaming with ecstasy and writhing beneath him. Then, she was coming again, the walls of her sex clenching around his cock. Dipping his head, he closed his teeth over one taut nipple, worrying that little bud while Goldi clawed at his back with a greedy pleasure.

Thrusting deeply into her, her pussy milking his cock, he came in a rush. He shot deep inside her, filling her up with it. The wet heat on his cock became almost unbearable.

Goldi cried out again, a fresh wave of contractions in her pussy signaling another orgasm.

Brent smiled against her breast, cuddling her close and savoring the perfection of having her as theirs.

Chapter 12

7 ½ months later

Goldi awoke with a slight pain in her stomach. Taking a deep breath, she relaxed and it went away. Noticing the guys must have already gotten up and she lay alone in the huge bed, she slowly rolled to her side and struggled to a sitting position. Waddling into the kitchen, following the scent of food, she saw Ben was fixing eggs.

"Good morning, sweetie! You should have stayed in bed. I was going to bring you breakfast," Ben greeted her while grinning. Goldi smiled back at him as she sat down at the table. The smile soon turned to a grimace as another pain shot through her stomach, this time lasting a little longer. Goldi took deep breaths while placing her hands on her huge, round tummy. Eventually the pain passed.

"Is something wrong?" Ben asked.

"It's nothing to worry about. Just a few small contractions. Are the eggs done because I'm starving?"

Ben brought over a plate filled with eggs and set it down in front of her.

Goldi quickly devoured the eggs, feeling like she hadn't eaten in forever. She was just finishing them when Brent and Brad came through door.

They walked over to her, each one kissing her on the cheek.

"Good morning. We've just put the finishing touches on the new nursery," Brent announced as he pulled up a seat at the table.

"Good morning honey," Brad said to her while taking the remaining chair.

"Goldi is having some contractions," Ben informed his brothers.

"Then — why are we sitting here? Brad go get her bag!" Brent ordered.

Brad started to get up from the table.

"Stop! It's not time yet," Goldi announced reassuringly.

"Just sit back down. Everything is fine; really."

"Are you sure?" Brad asked.

"Yes," Goldi replied, offering a smile. It was soon replaced with a look of pain when another contraction hit. This one even harder and lasting longer than the last. She doubled over as she tried to breathe in and out until it passed.

"That's it! We're taking you to the hospital," Brent ordered.

Immediately, Brad ran to go grab her packed bag, as Ben got up and grabbed the keys to the truck.

"Really, guys, it's all right! It's way too early to go to the hospital and the doctor said some pain is normal," Goldi responded.

"I've got the truck pulled up," Ben interjected as he came back into the cabin.

"I've got her bag in the back of the truck," Brad added.

"Then, we will be early," Brent informed Goldi as he held out his hand to help her up from her seat.

Knowing now there would be no use arguing, Goldi sighed in defeat and placed her hand in Brent's, so he could help her to her feet. It was reaching the point where she felt like they needed to invest in a crane. Just as she reached an upright position, she felt a gush of water between her legs as another contraction hit.

"Shit! Your water just broke," Brent cursed. Through clenched teeth, Goldi finally agreed, "Now it's time." Brent swept her up into his arms and carried her to the truck, settling her on the seat.

Brad and Ben climbed in from the driver's side, getting into the smaller seats in the back of the extended cab.

Hurriedly, Brent climbed into the truck and stepped on the gas, speeding toward the hospital.

When they reached the small hospital, the contractions were coming almost non-stop. Goldi couldn't help but to cry out in pain.

Ben, who sat the closest to her, took her hand in his. "Squeeze it as hard as you need to, Goldi."

"Remember your breathing," Brad told her while demonstrating the technique they'd learned together in class. If she wasn't in so much pain, she probably would've laughed at how these three hunky, manly guys were all flustered because she was in labor. "Just hurry!" she shouted between contractions. Brent did just that.

~*~*~

Goldi lay in the bed exhausted after giving birth. She gazed over to see Brent holding the baby girl while Brad and Ben each had one of the boys. She smiled weakly. How perfect it was that each of them had a baby in their arms! Another smile, they were definitely going to have their hands full with the triplets. Soon, they would have to come up with names for the new members of the Bear family but for now, she wanted nothing more than to just sleep.

Her baby girl seemed to have other ideas and began to whimper.

Brent got up and walked over to Goldi. "I think she's hungry," he suggested as he handed her the baby.

Goldi took the little girl into her arms and cradled her as she used her other hand to guide her nipple into the baby's hungry mouth.

Brent smiled lovingly down at them.

Goldi could feel the love coming from him, from all three of them.

"You've never been more beautiful, than you are right now," he said as he gently kissed her forehead.

"Then, you need your eyes checked because I'm a hot mess right now," Goldi replied flippantly.

"No. My eyes are perfect and you are the most gorgeous, lovely woman I have ever laid my eyes on and I wouldn't have you any other way."

Goldi fought to hold back her tears. She felt so blessed to be loved so deeply and completely. "I love you," she choked out.

~*~*~

"I love you," Brent replied and he meant every word of it. Only a few short months ago, if someone had told him that he would love Goldi more than his own life, he would've thought they were crazy. Watching her with the baby, he felt even more love for her and he knew his love would just keep growing as the years passed. How he ever got so lucky was beyond him, but he felt thankful every day to have her in his life.

Goldi peered down at the baby girl she held who'd now fell fast asleep and she kissed her sweet little cheek. "What shall we name you?"

"She's beautiful like her mother. So, why don't we name her Fayre," Brent suggested.

"Fayre Bear. I like it. What do the two of you think?" she asked Brad and Ben.

Brad came over to the bed holding the newborn baby boy. Standing next to Brent, he looked down at the baby girl Goldi held. "I agree she is beautiful like her mother, the name fits."

Ben also came over to the bed, taking up a spot next to Brad, the third baby nestled in his arms. "I agree."

"Then Fayre Bear it is. Now, we just need to name our two boys," Goldi reminded them.

Brad gazed down at the baby he held. "He's strong and a fighter, so how about Mark?"

"Mark Bear. Sounds good," Ben agreed.

"I like it." Brent nodded.

"Then, Mark Bear it is, my strong boy," Goldie replied as she reached out and gently touched the baby's head.

"My baby may be the smallest, but he's a little warrior. How about Sloan?" Ben asked.

"I like it," Brent and Brad replied at the same time, as was their habit.

"Sloan Bear it is," Goldi's reply sounded muted as she began drifting into an exhausted sleep.

Brent took Fayre from Goldi's arms and went back to the rocking chair.

Mark and Sloan started to fuss, so Brad and Ben quickly went out to the nurse's station, so they wouldn't wake poor Goldi. In just a few moments, they came back in...each holding a bottle for the baby, so they could feed them.

The bothers sat there, each holding a baby in their arms while grinning from ear to ear. None of them could believe how lucky they were to have Goldi in their lives and now to have three beautiful healthy babies to call their own.

At last, the Bear family was complete.

LEIGH SAVAGE

Leigh Savage lives in Saint Louis, MO with her husband and two children. Leigh is known for her paranormal erotic romance novels Angel of Death and Shadows of My Past.
"I grew up loving to escape in the world of stories that my Father would write just for me. So, it wasn't any wonder that as I got older, I too picked up the pen and started writing."

Follow Me On...

Facebook Fan Page: http://www.facebook.com/groups/leighsavage/

Facebook: http://www.facebook.com/AuthorLeighSavage

Amazon: amazon.com/author/leighsavage

GoodReads: http://www.goodreads.com/leighsavage

Made in the USA
Charleston, SC
02 July 2015